Dear Parent:
Your child's love of reading starts here!

Every child learns to read in a different way and at his or her own speed. Some go back and forth between reading levels and read favorite books again and again. Others read through each level in order. You can help your young reader improve and become more confident by encouraging his or her own interests and abilities. From books your child reads with you to the first books he or she reads alone, there are I Can Read Books for every stage of reading:

SHARED READING
Basic language, word repetition, and whimsical illustrations, ideal for sharing with your emergent reader

BEGINNING READING
Short sentences, familiar words, and simple concepts for children eager to read on their own

READING WITH HELP
Engaging stories, longer sentences, and language play for developing readers

READING ALONE
Complex plots, challenging vocabulary, and high-interest topics for the independent reader

ADVANCED READING
Short paragraphs, chapters, and exciting themes for the perfect bridge to chapter books

I Can Read Books have introduced children to the joy of reading since 1957. Featuring award-winning authors and illustrators and a fabulous cast of beloved characters, I Can Read Books set the standard for beginning readers.

A lifetime of discovery begins with the magical words "I Can Read!"

Visit www.icanread.com for information
on enriching your child's reading experience.

Justice League: Battle of the Power Ring
Copyright © 2016 DC Comics.
JUSTICE LEAGUE and all related characters and elements are trademarks of and © DC Comics.
(s16)

HARP34441
Manufactured in the U.S.A.
No part of this book may be used or reproduced in any manner whatsoever without written permission except
in the case of brief quotations embodied in critical articles and reviews. For information address HarperCollins
Children's Books, a division of HarperCollins Publishers, 195 Broadway, New York, NY 10007.
www.icanread.com

Library of Congress catalog card number: 2015943578
ISBN 978-0-06-234494-6

Book design by Victor Joseph Ochoa

16 17 18 19 20   LSCC   10 9 8 7 6 5 4 3   ❖   First Edition

I Can Read!

READING WITH HELP 2

JUSTICE LEAGUE

BATTLE OF THE POWER RING

by Donald Lemke
pictures by Patrick Spaziante

HARPER

An Imprint of HarperCollinsPublishers

GREEN LANTERN

Test pilot Hal Jordan is Green Lantern of Space Sector 2814. With his power ring, Green Lantern can create anything imaginable and guards Earth against the forces of evil.

SUPERMAN

Superman, also known as the Man of Steel, has many amazing superpowers. To hide his super hero identity, he works as reporter Clark Kent at the *Daily Planet* newspaper.

BATMAN

Orphaned as a child, young Bruce Wayne trained his body and mind to become Batman, the Dark Knight. He fights crime with high-tech gadgets and weapons.

THE FLASH

The Flash is also known as the Fastest Man Alive. With incredible speed, the lightning-quick super hero wastes no time taking down the world's worst villains.

DARKSEID

Darkseid is the ruler of the alien planet Apokolips and one of the most powerful beings in the universe.

DESAAD

Desaad is the chief scientist on Apokolips. He is also a loyal servant of Darkseid, ready to perform his master's evil deeds.

On Apokolips, the planet's ruler, Darkseid, sat atop his throne. His servant, Desaad, approached. "After years, I've finally done it, Lord Darkseid," said Desaad.

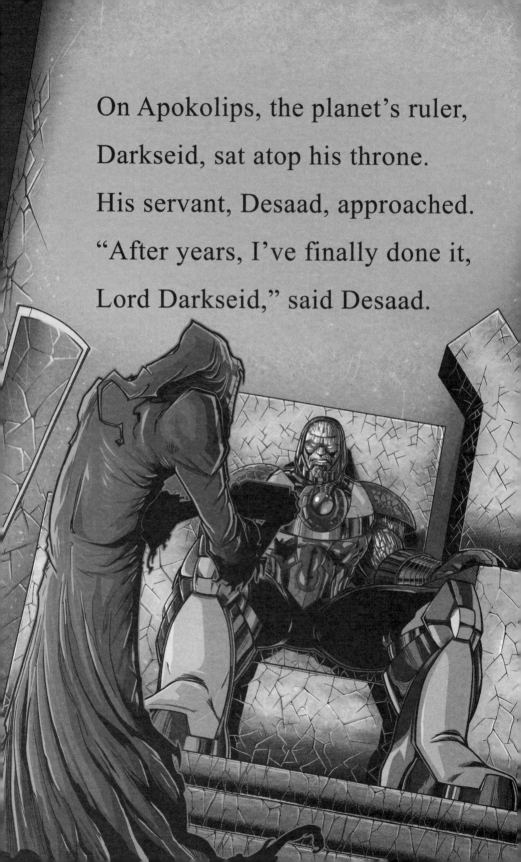

The servant held up a Mother Box.

A series of lights glowed on

the computer's small keypad.

"Behold, your newest weapon . . .

control of the Green Lanterns!"

"This device sends a signal to the planet Oa," Desaad said.
"It then connects to the Galactic Guardians' computer, and I can control every power ring."

"Correction," growled Darkseid,
as he snatched the Mother Box
from his servant.
"*I* will control them."
Darkseid typed in a number: 2814.

On Earth, Hal Jordan sat inside
a fighter jet at Ferris Aircraft.
He reached for the jet's controls,
but his right hand wouldn't move.
His Green Lantern power ring glowed.
It suddenly had a mind of its own!

"Ready for takeoff, Jordan?"
radioed the Ferris control tower.
But before he could respond,
the out-of-control ring pulled him
from the cockpit and into the sky.

Miles away, reporter Clark Kent sat
inside the Daily Planet Building,
awaiting his next big scoop.
Suddenly his boss shouted,
"Coast City is under attack . . .
by Green Lantern!"

Out of sight, Clark shed his suit,
revealing his Superman uniform.
ZOOM! In a red-and-blue blur,
the hero soared up, up, and away!

As Superman neared Coast City,
he saw Green Lantern high in the sky,
blasting the streets with his ring.
People fled in all directions.

14

"Hal!" shouted the Man of Steel.

"Hey, Superman," said Green Lantern.

"My ring is out of control!"

Suddenly the ring fired at Superman!

With his mighty fist, the super hero shattered the green beam.

Just then, The Flash and Batman arrived on the streets below.

"We thought you could use a hand," said the Fastest Man Alive.

"Another?" joked Hal. "I already have one more than I can handle!"

An oversized cannon grew from Green Lantern's out-of-control ring. *BOOM!* It shot green cannonballs at the Justice League members.

The Flash easily zigzagged
through the hail of cannonballs.
Batman fired his grapnel gun
at a nearby building,
zipping away from the explosions.

"Impressive," said a voice above.

The Justice League looked up.

"Darkseid," said Superman,

recognizing his worst enemy.

The villain floated above the city,

followed closely by Desaad.

"Do you like my toy?" asked Desaad.

"I call him my *Mean* Lantern!"

"That has a nice ring to it,"
The Flash joked.

"I assure you," replied Darkseid,

"that ring is anything but nice."

Instantly the power ring formed
three heat-seeking missiles.
The super heroes fled as the bombs
exploded into nearby buildings.

"Look at them run!" Desaad laughed. "They won't stand a chance against our Green Lantern army."

"Correction," said Darkseid, holding the Mother Box.

"*My* army."

Nearby, Green Lantern struggled
with his out-of-control power ring.
The ring struck him, over and over,
with a giant green boxing glove.
"Don't fight, mortal,"
Darkseid told him.
"I'm your master now."

23

"You may control my ring," said Hal, but you'll never control my will!" Green Lantern removed his ring, dropping the weapon at his feet. Without its wearer, the power ring quickly shut down.

"Fool!" cried Darkseid.

"You are nothing without that ring."

"Correction," said The Flash,

"He's a member of the Justice League."

The Flash darted at Darkseid,

landing fifty punches in a blink.

"No!" cried the evil ruler,

as the Mother Box fell from his hand.

"I don't have a ring," said Batman,
"but these bracelets should fit."
The Dark Knight held up a pair
of shiny metal Bat-Cuffs.
"Thanks, Batman," Hal said,
"but green is more his color."

Green Lantern picked up
the Mother Box and typed in
a familiar number: 0000.
A Boom Tube to the planet Oa
opened behind the villains.

The Man of Steel flew at Darkseid.
WHAM! With a mighty punch,
he sent the villain into the tube,
and Desaad followed closely behind.

Green Lantern placed his
power ring back on his right hand.
The ring glowed under his control,
but Green Lantern didn't smile.
"What's wrong?" asked The Flash.

"My ring may be fixed," said Hal,

"but my reputation is ruined."

He pointed at frightened onlookers

and the smoldering city around them.

"Have no fear, Hal," Superman said.
"Everyone will get the real
scoop soon enough."
The Man of Steel zoomed away,
heading back to the *Daily Planet*.